SPORTS DAY

Louise

Charles

Sara

William

Fred

First published in Great Britain by HarperCollins*Publishers* in 2000

1 3 5 7 9 10 8 6 4 2

ISBN: 000 664740-5

From the television series based on
the original Teddybear books
created by Alison Sage and Susanna Gretz.

Text adapted by Alison Sage
Illustrated by Stuart Trotter

Based on an original television series produced by United Productions
and Link Entertainment; Licensed by Link Licensing Ltd.
Text and illustrations © Link Entertainment and Meridian Broadcasting.

A CIP catalogue record for this title is available from the British Library.

The HarperCollins website address is:
www.**fire**and**water**.com

Printed and bound in Singapore

Sports Day

Collins

An imprint of HarperCollins*Publishers*

It was Saturday morning. All the bears were in the garden, and so was Fred the dog.

"Here! Fred!" said Louise. "Fetch!" She threw a stick for him.

Fred stared at the stick. He didn't move a paw. "Oh, FRED!" said Louise, crossly.

"I'll fetch the stick," cried Robert jumping up and down.

"No, *I* will!" said Louise.

"Why don't you both have a race for it?" said Charles. "Ready, teddy, GO!"

Louise and Robert ran off.

Robert grabbed the stick first and ran back to
Charles. "The winner!" he crowed happily.
"Now I'll race William,"
cried Charles.
William looked worried.
"Er-um – something's
burning in the kitchen!"
he mumbled, and
he ran off indoors.
"I can't smell
anything!" said Robert.
"What's the matter with him?"

"Dunno. But let's have a
Sports Day!" cried Sara.
"We can have all kinds of
races–"

"–and prizes!" added
Robert.

First, they got into their sports clothes.

"Now for the warm-up exercises," said Charles.

"But I'm not cold!" said Robert.

Louise giggled. "Don't be silly. You have to do warm-ups before you do a race."

Soon they were bending and jumping and hopping on the spot.

"Can we stop now?" puffed Louise. "I think I'm TOO warm."

It took a little while to get everything ready.

Sara got the tape measure out of the sewing basket and tied it to the bushes in the garden for a finishing line.

"Where's my stop watch? I'll be the starter and time everyone!" cried Charles.

"Let's have a sack race, too!" cried Sara.

Louise went into the kitchen.

"William! Why aren't you helping with Sports Day?" she asked.

"I'll boil some eggs," offered William. "For the egg and spoon race."

"What races are *you* going to do?" said Louise.

"I'm a bit busy at the moment," said William, looking worried.

Outside in the garden Sara found some sacks. "Where's William?" she asked, counting them. "I need a partner for the three-legged race."

"He says he's too busy," said Louise.

"Too busy?" said Charles. "The three-legged race will be spoiled if you haven't got a partner, Sara."

"Let's practise," said Robert to Louise. "Give me a paw, and we'll tie ourselves together."

This wasn't easy. Robert started to run. Taken by surprise, Louise toppled over and Robert fell flat on his face.

"You're so silly," he grumbled.

In the kitchen, William was eating the last of the biscuits. He could hear everyone laughing in the garden.

"I wish I was good at sport," he sighed.

Just then, Sara ran into the kitchen.

"Hurry up, William!" she cried. "Why aren't you joining in?"

She saw the empty packet of biscuits.

"William! You've eaten the prizes!"

William hung his head.

"I'm just no good at sport and – oh! – the eggs! They're boiling over!"

He raced to the stove.

"WILLIAM!" shrieked Sara.

"What have I done?" said William guiltily.

"If you can run like that," said Sara, "you're going to be my partner in the three-legged race!" And she marched him out into the garden.

"Are you sure about this?" said William, as they slowly hopped to the starting line.

"Very sure," said Sara.

"*We're* going to win, aren't we, Louise?" said Robert. "We've been *practising*."

They all set off like furry cannonballs.

Then Fred bounded up to join the fun.

"Get OFF, Fred!" spluttered Louise.

But Robert missed his footing, and he and Louise rolled over and over.

William and Sara kept running. They dodged Robert and Louise.

They hopped round Fred — and they flopped
over the winning line.

"THE WINNERS!" shouted Charles.
"Well done, William and Sara!"

"That was easy!" said William, grinning.

"You won't win the next one," said Robert.

"It's the sack race."

"Ready – Teddy – GO!!" yelled Charles.

"Sara's going well – and so
is Robert… oh, dear!
A problem with Robert's
sack… stop laughing Louise!
You won't win if you
giggle all the time!

"But look at William! He's storming in!"

William bounced first over the line.

"It's not fair!" said Robert. "Fred's old bone was in my sack."

"Never mind," said Sara. "Maybe you'll win the next race."

"It's the egg and spoon race!" cried Charles.

"Ready – Teddy – GO!!"

Sara went into the lead. Robert was chasing her and Louise was catching up fast.

But William hadn't given up. He was holding his egg steady.

Then Sara's egg got a wobble.

"Hold on Sara!" shouted Charles.

But Sara's egg wobbled so much that soon she was wobbling too.

"SARA!" yelled Robert. Sara had wobbled right in front of him and their eggs went flying.

Louise doubled up with laugher and dropped her spoon.

William grinned and crossed the finishing line.

"The winner! Again!" cried Charles. "Where's the prize biscuits?"

"William ate them!" said Sara.

"But I made some more for all of us," said William. "And see! I've got another prize."

He took his egg off his spoon and started to eat it. "Yummy!"

Louise

Charles

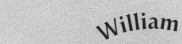
William

Sara

Fred

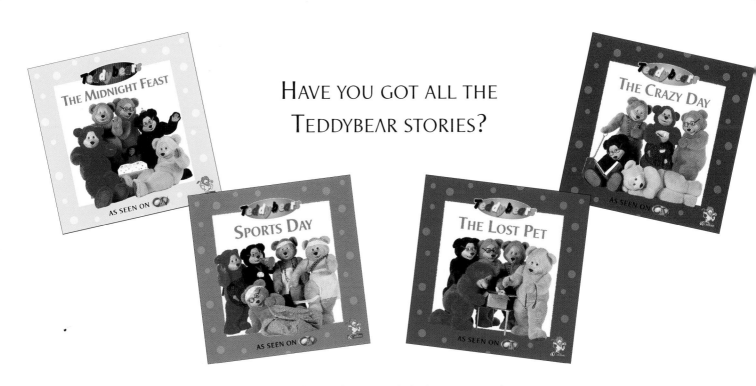

HAVE YOU GOT ALL THE
TEDDYBEAR STORIES?

Look out for the Teddybear videos too,
from all good video stockists.

Don't miss the new video *Giant Tomato and Other Stories*.